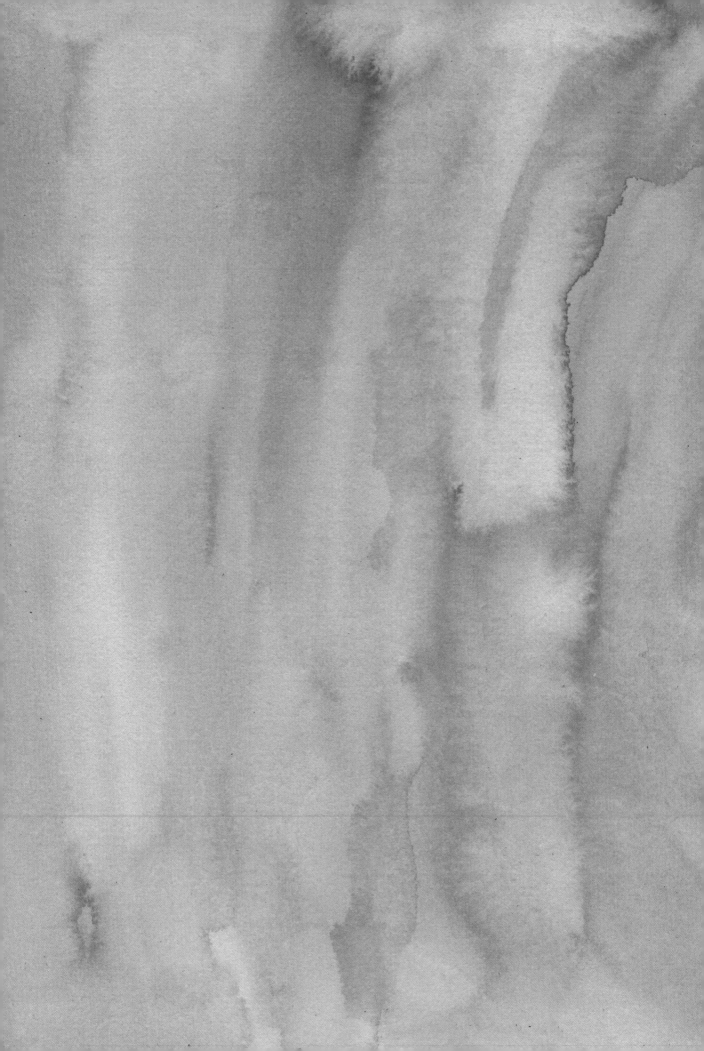

While Grandpa Naps

Written by
Naomi Danis

Illustrated by
Junghwa Park

Brooklyn, NY

Grandpa comes
to visit on Sunday.
He brings salami,
rye bread, mustard,
and pickles for
the whole family.

I can smell the salami
when I give him a hug.

Grandpa used to come together with Grandma Sarah, but she died, so now he comes alone. Sometimes Grandpa is sad. Sometimes Mom is sad too. And sometimes so am I.

After lunch Grandpa likes to rest in the hammock in our back yard.

I like the hammock too, but I always fall out of it. Dad told me I have to get into the hammock slowly.

I never told Dad I like falling out of the hammock.

But Grandpa doesn't fall out of the hammock. He's good at doing things slowly. He smiles at me.

"How's my boy?" Grandpa says. "How's my favorite boy?"

I don't know what to say. I think about my brothers. I wonder, does Grandpa say the same thing to Ricky and Billy?

"I'm okay," I answer Grandpa. I don't say, "You're my favorite Grandpa," even though he is actually my only Grandpa. Instead I say, "I love you, Grandpa."

"Gilbert—bring a chair
to sit next to me.
Be a good boy.
You make sure no flies
bother Grandpa while
he naps. Okay?"

"Okay, Grandpa,"
I say.

If a mosquito comes to buzz in Grandpa's ears, I will snap and clap at it.

If a fly comes stepping with its sticky feet across Grandpa's bald forehead—whoosh—I will blow it away

If an ant comes crawling from his shoes up his pants leg I will gently brush it, push it off.

I'm wearing my favorite shirt that Grandma and Grandpa bought for all the cousins when they went on vacation.

Maybe I am wearing Billy's shirt or Ricky's shirt, or maybe cousin Robby's shirt or cousin Barry's shirt.

FLORIDA

Mom said I am lucky. There will always be another bigger one of my favorite shirt and I will never outgrow it.

I don't know what Grandma and Grandpa brought cousin Carol or cousin Deanna.

Billy and Ricky come
running through the backyard.
"Tag, you're it," Billy shouts at Ricky.
Ricky turns to me and yells,
"Hey Gilbert, want to play?
You could be IT!"

But they keep running around to the
front of the house and I don't get to
explain that Grandpa is counting on
me, that I have a job to do.

If I did play tag with
them I think I might
turn out to be the
fastest runner, even
if I am the youngest
brother.

It's a long warm
summer afternoon.

After a while I notice no insects have been bothering Grandpa so I find myself a stick and poke around in the crumbly dirt looking for creepy crawling insects to keep away from Grandpa.

I find some bugs and beetles, but even better I find some wriggling worms.

Before I know it from looking and looking at them I feel my restless self wriggling and wiggling, just like the worms in the earth.

It isn't easy, but somehow I stay on my chair.

Mom calls from the kitchen window, "Want some watermelon Gilbert?"

I want the watermelon.

But I think I shouldn't leave Grandpa and I don't want
to wake him up by calling loudly back to Mom.

So I sit in my chair and I don't say anything.
I shake my head yes, but Mom can't hear that.

Out of the corner of my eye
I spy our neighbor's cat
creeping through our yard

step after step,
slowly, silently, stealthily,
all focused and intent on....

what could it be?

I find myself quietly following
the cat stepping slowly too,

and then suddenly-squawk
-a surprised bird flutters...

The cat sulks
and scampers off
and I hurry back to my seat.

Grandpa is snoring softly.
I wonder if he is dreaming
about Grandma Sarah.

I remember how she
used to pull little combs
out of her hair,

shake her head,
run her fingers
through her long
silvery hair,

twist it around
and around
on top of her
head and put
the combs
back in.

I look at the sky
where the white
and gray clouds
are not sitting still.

They are floating
slowly by, changing
shapes against the
sunny bright blue.

If a lot of clouds
gather, and the sky
turns gray, I will be
ready to protect
Grandpa from the
raindrops.

I know where to find a big beach umbrella because I helped Mom take everything out of the garage to find my old crib to get ready for the new baby.

I think about the watermelon again. I can see Mom through the kitchen window.

She is going to have the new baby after the summer.

If she has a girl we are going to name her Sarah to help us remember Grandma.

I will be in kindergarten when the baby comes. Mom says I will be so big then.

GILBERT

Dad comes home from the drugstore where he works on Sundays too. He comes into the backyard to say hello and finally Grandpa wakes up.

Grandpa looks surprised
to see me still sitting
next to him, watching
for flies.

"Thank you Gilbert.
You did a good job,"
he says, smiling.

"What a boy we got here,"
Grandpa says to Dad, shaking his head,
and patting my cheek.

He laughs in a way that I can tell he wants
me to laugh along with him.

"He watched so no flies would bother me while I
slept. He watched and watched." Grandpa laughs.

"Now, Gilbert,
let's all have some watermelon.
You deserve it."

"Yes!" I say to Grandpa.
And I laugh with him.

We all eat our watermelon.
Grandpa tells again how I
watched and watched him.
And we all laugh together.
When a story is good
you want to tell it again.

In memory of
Gil Oberfield,
with love for
our grandchildren.
–Naomi

For my grandfather
in heaven.
–Junghwa

While
Grandpa
Naps

Text © 2019 by Naomi Danis
Illustrations © 2019 by Junghwa Park

Published by POW! a division of
powerHouse Packaging & Supply, Inc.
32 Adams Street,
Brooklyn, NY 11201-1021
info@powkidsbooks.com
www.powkidsbooks.com
www.powerHouseBooks.com
www.powerHousePackaging.com

Printed and bound by Asia Pacific Offset

Book design by Krzysztof Poluchowicz

Library of Congress Control Number:
2018966645

ISBN: 978-1-57687-909-2

10 9 8 7 6 5 4 3 2 1

Printed in China

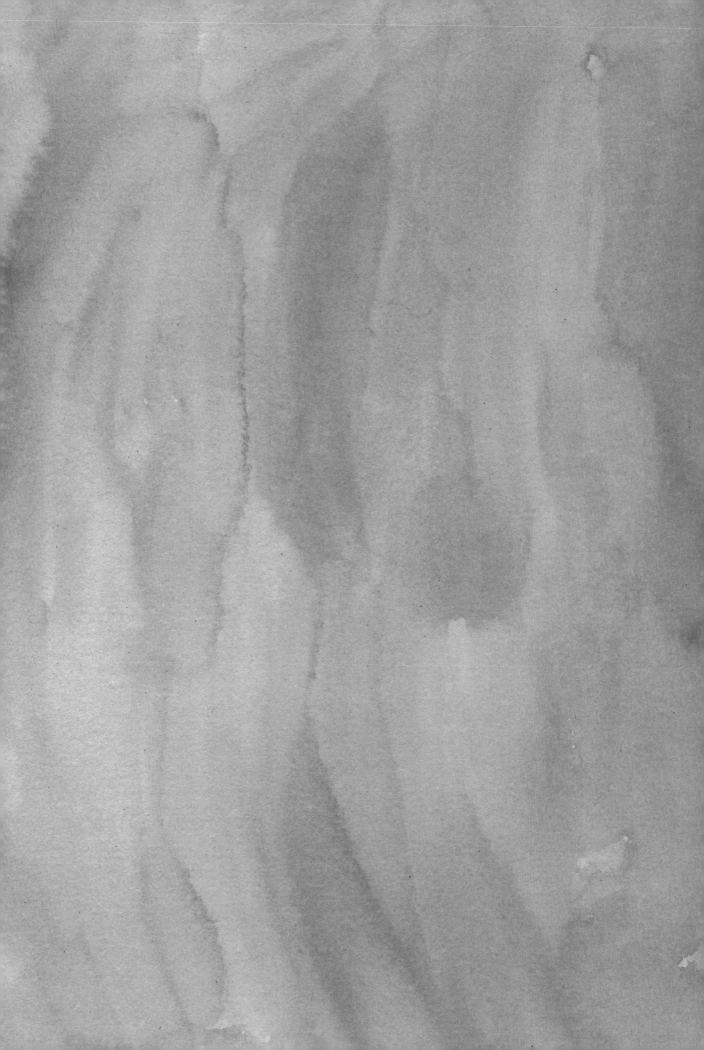